Ruby Gloom®
#1 Midnight Mystery

Ruby Gloom

#1 Midnight Mystery

By Rebecca McCarthy

Illustrated by Artful Doodlers

Grosset & Dunlap

GROSSET & DUNLAP
Published by the Penguin Group
Penguin Group (USA) Inc., 375 Hudson Street, New York, New York 10014, USA
Penguin Group (Canada), 90 Eglinton Avenue East, Suite 700, Toronto, Ontario
M4P 2Y3, Canada (a division of Pearson Penguin Canada Inc.)
Penguin Books Ltd., 80 Strand, London WC2R 0RL, England
Penguin Group Ireland, 25 St. Stephen's Green, Dublin 2, Ireland
(a division of Penguin Books Ltd.)
Penguin Group (Australia), 250 Camberwell Road, Camberwell, Victoria 3124,
Australia (a division of Pearson Australia Group Pty. Ltd.)
Penguin Books India Pvt. Ltd., 11 Community Centre, Panchsheel Park, New
Delhi—110 017, India
Penguin Group (NZ), 67 Apollo Drive, Rosedale, North Shore 0632, New Zealand
(a division of Pearson New Zealand Ltd.)
Penguin Books (South Africa) (Pty.) Ltd., 24 Sturdee Avenue,
Rosebank, Johannesburg 2196, South Africa

Penguin Books Ltd., Registered Offices: 80 Strand, London WC2R 0RL, England

www.rubygloom.com

Library of Congress Control Number: 2007040892

ISBN 978-0-448-44672-1   10 9 8 7 6 5 4 3 2 1

Dear Friend,

Welcome to Gloomsville!

I live in a Victorian mansion with all of my friends. I can't wait for you to meet them. They mean the world to me.

There's Iris, a one-eyed girl who loves going on wild adventures; Skull Boy, who's always trying to figure out who he's descended from; Frank and Len, brothers that share a body and a love of loud music; Poe, a really smart crow; Misery, a girl with the worst luck in the world; Scaredy Bat, a little bat who's afraid of everything; Boo Boo, a ghost who isn't the least bit scary; and Doom Kitty, my best friend.

I like to think that I know my friends pretty well, but every once in a while they surprise me! Like this one time when we all had fun solving a mystery in the mansion. The key to solving it was remembering that things aren't always what they seem.

Like I always say, never judge a book by its cover (it's the inside that counts)!

Enjoy our story!

Your friend, **Ruby**

P.S. I almost forgot! I'm Ruby Gloom—the happiest girl in the world!

Chapter One

"Don't be sad because roses
have thorns, be glad
because thorns have roses!"

The moon shone brightly as evening fell
upon the old Victorian mansion at the edge of
Gloomsville. It was so bright that Ruby Gloom
decided not to light the candles on the large,
rectangular table in the Great Hall. *Tonight we'll
dine by moonlight!* she thought.

As she set the table, she passed a mirror on
the wall and noticed her reflection. The blue
moonlight made her bright red hair look purple.
Her fair, freckled skin looked blue, and her
orange and yellow striped tights looked green. She
giggled at the sight of herself in the eerie light.

After all, Ruby was the cheeriest person in the world.

When the grandfather clock chimed seven times, the thick doors of the Great Hall opened slightly. Misery shuffled in, with her usual tired-looking expression. Her long, black hair fell all the way to the floor, and her drab, purple dress dragged on the floor as she walked. She carefully carried a small, white ceramic bowl with both hands.

"Hey, Ruby," she said in her low, gravelly voice. "I finally finished making a new sugar bowl to replace the one I dropped last week." Misery always had the worst luck. In fact, every single person in Misery's family tree had bad luck.

"It's beautiful!" Ruby said cheerfully.

"It took me all week to make it," Misery said as she continued toward the dining table. "I shaped the clay, I let it dry, I fired it, I painted it, and then I fired it again. I'm going to be extra careful this time and not let anything bad hap—"

Ruby gasped as Misery stumbled over a floorboard and the bowl went flying forward. The bowl broke into dozens of pieces and sugar spilled everywhere. Once Misery stood back up, she looked at the broken bowl.

"Hmm," she said without the least bit

of shock. "I guess I'll be making another bowl tonight. Let's see . . . that'll be bowl number 342."

"That's the spirit," Ruby said encouragingly. "If at first you don't succeed, try, try 342 more times!" Misery nodded, sighed, and took a seat near the middle of the table.

Just then, Frank and Len came in through the open door. They eagerly made for the dining table and nearly tripped over each other's foot.

Sometimes it could be difficult to share a body—especially since Len wasn't quite as good at paying attention to details. But when it came to style and making music, they were a perfect team. Both brothers loved wearing punk-rock clothes and playing extremely loud music.

Ruby brightened upon seeing the brothers. "Hey, I heard you guys rehearsing in the garage while I was setting the table. It sounded great! Was that a new song?"

"Oh, we weren't rehearsing," Frank said.

"Right," Len added. "We were just moving the furniture!"

Ruby giggled and placed a basket filled with warm buns on the table.

Next, Scaredy Bat entered the room. The tiny bat looked around with his large, innocent eyes, his one single fang chattering nervously. Despite being a bat, Scaredy was afraid of flying . . . and the dark. In fact, Scaredy was pretty much afraid of everything.

Just then, the door closed behind Scaredy with a clunk. He shrieked and dove underneath the carpet.

"Scaredy," Ruby said softly, "that was just the door closing behind you. Nothing to be afraid of." Scaredy Bat wiggled his way out from under the rug. "Oh. Yes, yes, of course," he said with his musical accent. "But you must admit, the sound of those doors is quite alarming."

Just then, a small, chubby-cheeked ghost rose up through the floor, right behind Scaredy Bat, and shouted, "Boo!"

"AAAAH!!" screamed Scaredy Bat as he dove back under the rug.

Ruby was delighted to see

her friend Boo Boo, the ghost-in-training, and she smiled to greet him. She bent down toward where Scaredy Bat was hiding. "Don't be afraid. It's just Boo Boo," she said.

"What?!" the adorable little ghost protested. "Be VERY afraid! I'm a big, scary, awful, terrible, spooooooky ghost!" Boo Boo crossed his arms and pouted.

Ruby couldn't help but smile. He was as cute as a cupcake. No matter how hard he tried, the only person he could manage to scare was Scaredy—and that wasn't saying much.

"You all right, Scaredy?" she asked the little lump under the rug. Again, Scaredy Bat wiggled out. He looked up and saw Boo Boo, who appeared to be very proud of himself.

"Oh, Boo Boo," Scaredy laughed. "You are becoming most expert at the art of scaring other creatures. Once again you have, as they say, 'gotten me.'" Boo Boo and Scaredy made their way over to the dining table together, and greeted the others as they took their seats.

"Has anyone seen Poe?" Ruby asked. "He's always on time." Poe was a most unusual crow who lived with his brothers, Edgar and Allen, just outside the mansion in a cozy coop. He was very refined and spent most of his time listening to opera and reading poetry. He even claimed to be descended from the great writer Edgar Allan Poe's pet bird, Paco.

"Oh yeah, we forgot to tell you, we saw him when we walked over from the garage," Frank said.

"He said to tell everyone he won't be joining us for dinner tonight," Len continued.

"Really? Did he say why?" Ruby asked curiously.

"I dunno, something about a moment of inspiration, beginning work of epic proportions, not wanting to interrupt the flow of his startling genius something-or-other, blah blah blah," Len said as he poured himself a cup of juice.

"Well, we'll save him some leftovers," Ruby decided, "in case he gets hungry later."

Next, Skull Boy walked through the double doors. He had a small, white towel around his neck, and wore a warm-up suit with sneakers. He breathed out deeply and sank into a seat at the very end of the table.

"Hi, Skull Boy." Ruby smiled warmly. "You look a little down today. Everything okay?"

Skull Boy smiled as he looked up at his friend, but he

couldn't hide his true feelings. "Well," he said, "I spent the day outside, running laps around the mansion. I thought that I might be related to the great Sir Roger Bannister. He was the first person ever to run a mile in under four minutes. I ran a mile, then I ran another mile, and then I ran another mile, but I just couldn't break four minutes and zero point one seconds. Guess running's just not in my blood." He sighed. "Well, at least I got some great exercise today, so it wasn't a total waste of time."

As Ruby took a seat, Doom Kitty jumped swiftly from the floor to the table. Then she took her seat next to the saucer of milk that Ruby had set out for her. Doom was Ruby's best friend—they even shared a room.

"Doom," Misery said, "don't you know it's bad

luck for a black cat to cross a person's path?"
Doom glanced back at Misery and yawned, as
if to say, "Oh, you don't really believe that silly
superstition, do you?" Then suddenly there was
a *crash* and a *bang*! From out in the hallway
they heard a *whirly-whip, rumble, tumble clang
bada-bang*!

"I'm good!"
Iris said as she
pushed the door
open and entered
the Great Hall.
In her hands she
carried a small
flower by the

roots. "Look what I found!" she announced.
Iris had straight, short black hair and one very
large eye in the middle of her forehead. She was
always going off on wild adventures, and it was
no surprise that she had once again come back

with a souvenir. As her friends gathered around, she said proudly, "I sure do have an eye for beauty, if I do say so myself!"

"That is the most beautiful flower I've ever seen!" Ruby exclaimed.

"Whoa—cool flower!" Frank and Len said at the same time.

"What a most interesting sample of flora," said Scaredy.

"It looks just like the corsage my great, great, great grandmother wore to dinner with the captain aboard the *Titanic*," marveled Misery. Then she added, "Before it sank." It seemed as if everyone Misery was related to had played some role in the world's biggest disasters.

"Where are you going to keep it, Iris?" asked Ruby.

"How about your room?" Iris suggested. "You get the most sunlight in the mansion, and it would look beautiful on your windowsill."

Ruby smiled widely. "Oh, I'd love to keep it in my room! I promise I'll water it every day and even play music for it when I'm gone."

Frank and Len perked up. "You're gonna play music?" Frank asked.

"For your flower?" Len followed.

"Yes," Ruby said. "Botanists say that soft music helps plants and flowers grow."

"Really!" Frank exclaimed with surprise.

"You want us to bring our guitar over someday and play a tune for the little guy?" asked Len.

"Sure, that'd be great!" Ruby said. "But just make sure to keep it soft. Flowers don't react well to lots of noise." The brothers looked disappointed, but then shrugged.

"Okay, uh, we'll try. But 'soft' really isn't one of our strong points," said Frank. With the flower in hand, Ruby headed for the kitchen.

The sound of opening and closing cabinets

was heard, followed by the clunking of pots and bowls, the whoosh of running water, the shoveling of dirt, the snipping of scissors, the humming of a tune, and then *voila*! Ruby came back into the Great Hall with the heart-shaped flower neatly planted in a colorful pot. She placed the pot on a small table next to the fireplace and returned to the dining table.

"Well, everyone," she announced, "let's eat!"

Chapter Two

"Sometimes you
have to make your
own sunshine!"

The wind whispered softly against the
drapes as Ruby put on her nightgown and fluffy
bedroom slippers. She carried the new plant
over to her window
and gently
placed it
on the sill.
*Time for
bed, my
newest little
friend,* she
thought.

Doom rubbed up against Ruby's legs as she turned toward the bed. As Ruby stretched her arms way up into the air, Doom did the same. Ruby climbed into her bed and slid under the thick comforter, while Doom curled up in hers. After a few deep breaths both Ruby and Doom Kitty were fast asleep.

By the time the moon was high in the sky, everyone was asleep in the mansion—everyone except for Scaredy Bat. A strange noise had

woken him up. He tried to tell himself that the noise he had heard was just the wind. But then he heard a loud *bang* and a *bump*, followed by the creaking of doors and a strange slithering sound in the hallway. Now he was certain that what he had heard wasn't the wind. Scaredy pulled the covers over his eyes and shivered and shook until dawn.

The next morning was dreary and overcast—just the way Ruby liked it. She rubbed her eyes and looked out at the gray, cloudy sky and thought, *Well, it looks like Mr. Sun wants me to make my own sunshine today!* She slipped out of bed and walked toward the windowsill. Her eyes widened at the sight of her new little flower. It wasn't so little anymore!

Ruby clapped her hands. "You certainly are growing up nice and strong!" she said. "I'll bring you back some water after breakfast."

Ruby pulled on her orange and yellow striped tights and her favorite black dress, and headed for the kitchen. Doom followed close behind, stopping once to glance back at the flower. For a moment, it looked as though its leaves were waving good-bye. Doom shook her head, blinked several times, and then followed Ruby to the kitchen.

A low whisper of worried voices met Ruby's ears when she got to the kitchen. Questions such as, "Really? They're all gone?" and "But how can that be?" echoed through the hallway. Curious to know what all the fuss was about, Ruby sped toward the door and opened it. There she saw Skull Boy, Iris, Scaredy Bat, Misery, Frank and Len, and Poe all holding empty baskets and bowls, and peering inside the cabinets and cupboards. The table was set, but the plates and pitchers were empty.

"Thank goodness you're here," Poe said

when he saw Ruby. "Perhaps you can explain this most curious situation."

"I'll try. What's going on?" Ruby asked, and walked toward the group.

"It's horrible!" Misery exclaimed. "All the food has disappeared and now we're all going to starve!"

"We're not going to starve," Skull Boy said, "but it is strange that all the food is missing."

"What?" Ruby said, stunned. "But I just made a batch of muffins yesterday."

"And we had a lot of leftovers from dinner last night," Iris added.

Ruby crossed over to the cupboards and opened one. With the exception of Boo Boo popping out to say, "Boo!" it was empty. She then opened all the drawers, cabinets, and cupboards.

"Found something!" called Ruby as she searched the highest cabinet in the kitchen. "I don't suppose anyone would like a bowl of flour with a side of baking soda for breakfast?" Ruby joked, but nobody seemed to be in a laughing mood. "Don't worry, guys," she said, "I think I found enough ingredients to make a fresh batch of muffins and some bread. But it does seem that we have a mystery on our hands."

"And I'm just the person to solve it!" Skull Boy chimed in. "I've been reading all about Sherlock Holmes, and I think we may be related. If I can solve this mystery, it will prove that I

inherited some of his talent!"

Poe interrupted. "I'm sorry, Skull Boy, but you could not possibly be descended from Sherlock Holmes. He is a fictional character in a series of fictional books." Skull Boy's smile turned to a heavy frown.

"But," Poe hastily added, "you could be descended from Sir Arthur Conan Doyle. He wrote the Sherlock Holmes mysteries and therefore had a keen eye for detail and a talent for solving puzzles."

Skull Boy's face brightened once again and he picked up a nearby magnifying glass. "I must start searching for clues immediately!"

"Speaking of clues, Detective Skull Boy, sir," Scaredy said softly, "I am not sure this is of very much importance, but last night I was kept quite awake by some very strange sounds."

"Aha!" shouted Skull Boy excitedly. "The plot thickens!"

Skull Boy listened carefully as Scaredy explained about the banging and bumping noises he had heard last night. When Scaredy finished, Skull Boy stroked his chin and said, "Interesting. Very interesting, indeed. This is shaping up to be quite a mystery. I shall call it 'The Case of the Missing Foodstuffs' by Skull Boy, descendant of the famous Sir Arthur Conan Doyle! I must gather my detective kit at once."

As Skull Boy dashed out of the room, Iris turned to Ruby.

"Would you like some help making your muffins, Ruby?" she asked.

"Sure, Iris!" said Ruby. "Maybe you, Frank, and Len can go outside and pick some fresh berries to put in them."

"Great!" Iris said. "I know a meadow where blueberries grow as big as ping-pong balls." She and the brothers grabbed a couple of baskets and left.

"How about us, Ruby?" asked Boo Boo.

"Can we be of help?" added Scaredy Bat.

"Well," said Ruby, "there's a patch of dirt on the floor over by the doorway. I must have missed it when I swept the floor last night after dinner. Would you two mind sweeping it up?"

Scaredy Bat and Boo Boo stood proudly with their chests out and gave Ruby a salute. "Aye, aye, Captain!" they said playfully and turned toward the broom closet.

Seeing that everything was taken care of, Misery said, "Well, I guess I'll go to my room and start working on my new bowl. See you, Ruby. I'm sorry your muffins disappeared."

"Oh, that's okay." Ruby smiled. "I like baking treats for my friends! What could be more fun?"

"Hmm," Misery said thoughtfully. "Counting the cobwebs in the ceiling rafters—that's always a good time. Staring at the clock to count the minutes as the day goes by, watching the weeds grow, standing outside in the rain—that's fun. Except when lightning strikes you—that's no fun . . ." she muttered as she shuffled off to her room.

Chapter Three

"Sometimes the minor
details are of major
importance!"

Skull Boy looked at his reflection in his
mirror. He wore a brown and white checker-
patterned vest and pants, a pair of brown
boots, and a cap with a visor in the front and
also the back. He held a magnifying glass in
one hand. He lifted the magnifying glass to his
eye and said, "Elementary, my dear Watson.
Elementary." Now Skull Boy completely looked
and sounded the part of Sherlock Holmes.

He entered the kitchen just as Ruby was
leaving to allow her loaf of bread dough to
rise. Boo Boo and Scaredy Bat had already

finished sweeping up the dirt on the floor by the doorway. They were about to begin sweeping another area near the pantry when Skull Boy stopped them.

"Wait! Don't clean that up yet. It could be a clue!" Scaredy and Boo Boo stopped, looked at each other, shrugged, and took a few steps back. They didn't want to interrupt Gloomsville's newest master detective at work.

"Mm-hmm . . . mm-hmm . . . I see . . . ," said Skull Boy as he examined the dirt through his magnifying glass. He picked up an object from the dirt. It looked like a hair bow. He put it in his bag and continued to examine the dirt. Scaredy and Boo Boo tried to catch a glimpse of the evidence.

"Looks like boring old dirt to me," Boo Boo said, just before he and Scaredy Bat left the room.

"There can be important clues in this boring old dirt," Skull Boy said aloud to the empty kitchen. Now that he was alone, nothing would get in the way of searching for more clues.

"Well, well, well, what have we here? Another clue?" Skull Boy said as he spotted a small object on the countertop. It was a guitar pick. Through the magnifying glass, Skull Boy could clearly see that it had the letters *RIP* engraved on the back. "The brothers acted as if they didn't know about the missing food this morning. Perhaps when I tell them that

I discovered a guitar pick with their band name on it they'll change their tune!" he said confidently.

Just then, something on the countertop caught Skull Boy's attention. The top drawer was open slightly, and there appeared to be a notebook inside. Skull Boy opened the drawer farther and gasped at what he saw. "Aha! Ruby's diary! It seems Miss Gloom will have some explaining to do."

The next clue Skull Boy found was a long feather quill with ink on the tip. "It appears as if Poe has been at the scene of the crime, too," Skull Boy noted.

Next he found a handkerchief with a large *M* embroidered on the corner. "There's only one girl in Gloomsville who carries such a hankie. And that's . . . Misery! Looks like I'll be doing a lot of interrogating today."

Skull Boy grandly swung his cape around

his shoulders and dashed for the door. Unfortunately, he tripped over the edge of the cape on the way and stumbled awkwardly to the floor. He landed unharmed, which was lucky, but he noticed something sticking out from underneath the doormat. It was a small bone. Skull Boy held up the magnifying glass. "It appears to be a distal phalanx of a little toe. Who in Gloomsville could have lost the distal phalanx of their . . ." Skull Boy gasped when he realized that the smallest bone in his own little toe was, indeed, missing. "Do you know what this means?" he said aloud. "It means I am also a suspect in the case! I'd better interrogate myself right away! Where was I on the night of the theft?"

Skull Boy quickly sat down in an empty chair and replied nervously, "I was in bed, resting soundly. I swear it!"

He stood, now facing the empty chair, and

continued to interrogate himself. "And yet, my distal phalanx was found right at the scene of the crime! How do I explain that?"

Sitting, he answered, "I . . . I got hungry in the middle of the night. I came down for a midnight snack. But I only had a small glass of milk and nothing more. Please, I gotta believe me!"

Skull Boy took a deep breath. "As a matter of fact, I do remember drinking a glass of milk last night, and tripping over the welcome mat on my way out. That must be how my bone got left behind."

He stood up and stroked his chin. He concluded, "Okay, well, I guess I'm telling the truth. I can go—but I better not leave town until this crime is solved."

Sitting down again quickly, Skull Boy said, "Okay, I promise!" With a sigh of relief at having cleared his own name, Skull Boy rose and headed out toward the meadow to question the other suspects.

Chapter Four

> "You gotta have a dream,
> you gotta have a goal . . . and
> you gotta have an alibi!"

In a nearby meadow, Skull Boy found Iris picking blueberries. "Come here to hide from the law, did you?"

"Huh?" Iris said with a start. She hadn't noticed that Skull Boy had come up behind her.

"I said," repeated Skull Boy as he looked Iris up and down with his magnifying glass, "come here to hide from the law, did you?"

"Um, actually, I was picking blueberries for Ruby," Iris said.

"Oh," said Skull Boy. It wasn't the answer he expected. "Well, would you care to explain how

I found *this* on the floor near one of the kitchen cupboards—precisely where last night's crime took place?"

Iris gasped when she saw her favorite hair bow. "There it is!" she said happily. "I've been looking all over for it. I need this to keep my hair out of my eye. It must have fallen out last night when I—"

"When you stole all the foodstuffs from the kitchen?" Skull Boy accused.

"No!" Iris protested. "I didn't do it. I just got hungry in the middle of the night and went down for a snack."

"Aha!" shouted Skull Boy.

"No, no 'aha.' I only took a handful of grapes," Iris insisted. "Then I went straight back upstairs to my room and jumped on my trampoline until I got tired enough to fall asleep. Promise!"

"A likely story," Skull Boy said. He wasn't sure he believed her, but he stomped off to question the other suspects, anyway.

Nearby, Frank and Len were humming a tune in not-so-perfect harmony as they picked blueberries off the shrubs. Their teeth and lips were blue, as more of the berries made it into their mouths than into the basket. Skull Boy snuck up behind them.

"Where were you late last night?" he demanded. Frank abruptly stopped singing, but Len was so absorbed in the music that he didn't hear Skull Boy at all. Len sang, "Hush, little flower, don't you cry, Lenny's gonna feed you a ham on rye—"

"Uh . . . Len," Frank interrupted, "flowers don't eat ham on rye sandwiches."

"Oh. Well, what do they eat?" Len asked innocently.

"I dunno," Frank said, "maybe ham on . . . soil? Detective Skull Boy, do you know?"

"Don't try to distract me from the task at hand," Skull Boy said as he eyed the brothers through his magnifying glass. "Now, where were you late last night?"

Frank and Len jumped back in fear. "Uh, we don't remember!" said Frank.

"It's all such a blur!" stuttered Len.

Skull Boy whipped out the quill pen from his bag and shouted, "Well, does *this* jog your memory?"

The brothers stared blankly at the quill and said, "Uh, no, not really."

"Oh. Wait." Skull Boy put the quill away and pulled out the guitar pick. "I meant *this*!"

The brothers gasped and took a step back. "But . . . but . . . how'd that get in there?" asked Frank. "We've never seen that before in our life!" Len said frantically.

"Really?" Skull Boy said, confused. This wasn't the response he planned on getting. "Okay, well, perhaps I was mistaken—"

"All right, I confess!" Len shouted. "I came to the kitchen for a midnight snack and I must have dropped the guitar pick along the way!"

Frank turned to Len and shook his head. "Len, how could you?"

Len continued his confession. "But don't blame my brother! He was asleep. I was the culprit! I ate that piece of toast all by myself!"

Skull Boy wrinkled his brow. "But you two

are attached. How could . . . ? I mean, how could Len . . . ? Without Frank knowing? Um . . ." Figuring out how Len could have been in the kitchen without Frank knowing was too difficult for Skull Boy to understand, so he shook his head and got back to the investigation.

"Wait a second. Did you say that you only ate one piece of toast?" he asked.

Len continued to confess. "Yes! Yes, I ate the whole piece! Cuff me! Take me away! Do what you will! But please spare my brother!"

Skull Boy exchanged a look with Frank. "Len," he said, "if you only ate one piece of toast, you're not guilty."

"Yes, I am!" Len insisted. "Take me to the big house! Take me to the joint! Take me to the slammer! I deserve to be put away for liiiiiife . . ." he whimpered while on his knees.

Frank turned to Skull Boy and said, "You got any other questions, Detective?"

"Nope. I think that covers it. Thanks, and good luck with the song," Skull Boy said and left the meadow.

As Skull Boy went back into the house to find Misery, he accidentally slipped in the foyer and crashed to the ground. "Ouch!" he exclaimed. "That's the second time today!" He looked up to see Ruby standing over him.

"Are you okay?" she said and offered him a hand. "You must have slipped on all this dirt."

"Oh, I'm fine," Skull Boy said, taking her hand. As he looked around, he realized a few of his bones lay scattered about the area. "Could you help me put all these back in?" he asked.

"Sure," Ruby said helpfully. She picked up a calf bone that had rolled to the edge of the rug. "Here's your fibula."

"Thanks. By the way, Ruby, I found your

diary in one of the drawers in the kitchen. Unfortunately, that places you at the crime scene, so I'm going to have to interrogate you as a prime suspect in the case."

"Okay," said Ruby cooperatively, "I think that'll be fun!" She snapped one of Skull Boy's metatarsals back into place in one of his fingers. Then she politely took a seat on a chair next to the wall. "Ready," she said.

Skull Boy turned out all the lights but one—a white spotlight, which he aimed directly at Ruby's face—and nodded. This was just how Skull Boy had seen it done in old movies. He took his place in front of her and pointed a finger at her nose. He shouted, "Where were you on the night the foodstuffs disappeared?"

Ruby struck a dramatic pose, grasping the chair with both hands. "All right, buster," she said, "you drive a hard bargain. I admit that I went to the kitchen for a bun last night, and it was delicious. Not only that, but I got to spend all morning today baking, and you know that's one of my favorite things to do. So I suppose you're thinking that makes me the thief." Ruby took a deep breath, threw her head back with a dramatic flair, and covered her forehead with the back of her hand. "Well, yeah, in a way I'm glad the food got stolen, see? Glad, I tell you! I had a terrific morning and I can't wait to do it again!" Then she made a fist and looked directly

into the light for the big finale. "But that doesn't make me a thief, Detective. I didn't eat all that food and you can't prove that I did."

Ruby let out a deep breath and blotted her eyes

with a handkerchief, as if she'd been crying. Skull Boy was impressed. Obviously, Ruby liked old movies as much as he did. She played the part perfectly! He turned the lights back on and clapped his hands, giving her a standing ovation. "That was terrific, Ruby!" he said. "One of the best interrogations yet!"

"Thanks!" she said, smiling. "Anyway, I better get back to my cleaning. I think Frank and Len must have tracked some dirt in from the meadow because I keep finding clumps everywhere."

"Actually," Skull Boy corrected, "they're still outside. I just questioned them."

"Oh, well then, maybe it was Doom. She's always getting into something."

"Maybe. See ya. I've got more suspects to interrogate," said Skull Boy as he headed for Misery's room.

Chapter Five

"Sometimes the
safest place to sleep is
under the bed."

The door to Misery's room seemed to be stuck. No matter how hard Skull Boy pushed and pulled, he could not get it open. "So much for surprise entrances and catching the suspect off guard," he said to himself, and knocked on the door.

Slowly, the heavy door cracked open. Skull Boy shivered as he entered the dusty, candlelit room flecked with cobwebs.

"Finally," Misery said. "I've been waiting for you to come and interrogate me." She sat at a table, staring at a misshapen lump of clay, and sighed. Skull Boy figured that this was the beginnings of her new bowl, to replace the one she broke last night.

"Yes, well, uh," he stammered. Misery's room always made him feel a little uneasy. "Did you do it?"

"No," she said directly. "Somebody beat me to it."

"Huh?" Skull Boy asked, confused.

"I got hungry and went downstairs for a bite, but when I got there, all the food was gone." Then she added flatly, "Figures."

"Here's your handkerchief," Skull Boy offered, pulling the embroidered handkerchief out of his bag.

"Thanks, Skull Boy, I must have left my handkerchief behind." He hadn't anticipated that this interrogation would go this smoothly.

"Okay, well, I'm gonna get going. Have fun making a new bowl out of that lump of clay."

Misery looked up at him and said, "That *is* my new bowl. I'm waiting for it to dry."

"Oh," Skull Boy said. "Interesting, uh, design."

And with that, Skull Boy exited Misery's room as quickly as possible.

Later, Skull Boy questioned Boo Boo. He

hadn't come up with any new information as to the thief's identity, but he did run into Ruby again. She was scrubbing a dirty staircase. As he stepped around the small piles of dirt, she commented, "Must have been Iris on another one of her adventures."

"Nope, Iris is still in the meadow with the brothers," Skull Boy said.

"Oh, well then, perhaps Misery . . ."

"Misery's in her room watching a clay bowl dry," Skull Boy added.

"Huh," said Ruby. "There sure are a lot of messes around the house today . . ."

After a long day of questioning suspects and searching for clues, Skull Boy finally arrived at Poe's coop. When Skull Boy rapped on Poe's door, he heard the rustling of papers inside. Then Poe swung the door open abruptly.

"What do you want? I'm very busy," Poe said with more than a little frustration.

"Where were you on the night of the crime?" Skull Boy responded quickly. He didn't want to waste Poe's valuable time.

"What crime?"

"The crime of the missing foodstuffs," Skull Boy reminded him.

"Oh, that crime."

"Yes."

"I was working," Poe stated proudly.

"Working on what?" Skull Boy inquired.

"Working on my work."

Skull Boy pulled the quill out of his bag and said, "Would

you care to explain how this quill made its way into the kitchen last night, sir?"

"I ran out of ink last night, so I flew over to the mansion to fetch another bottle. Ruby keeps them in a supply closet for me in the kitchen. I must have dropped my quill on the way out."

"Ha! You expect me to believe that?" Skull Boy exclaimed dramatically.

Poe remained calm and said, "It is an old maxim of mine that when you have excluded the impossible, whatever remains, however improbable, must be the truth. Sherlock Holmes said that."

"He did?" Skull Boy said. His interest was piqued.

"He did. Now, are there any further questions? I really must return to my work."

"Yes. Would a flower eat a ham on rye sandwich?"

"Possibly," Poe responded without a second's

thought. "It depends on the flower. Most don't eat at all. They absorb nutrients and water through their roots in the ground. Though there are exceptions. A Venus flytrap eats flies, for example."

"Thank you."

"You're welcome."

"Well, see you later!" Skull Boy smiled.

"Good day, sir," Poe said and then closed the door firmly. Skull Boy returned to the mansion with his case still unsolved, but at least he had learned some very interesting plant facts!

Chapter Six

"Lions and tigers and
flowers, oh my!"

Going to sleep that night was difficult for
everyone except Ruby. She was tired from all the
baking and cleaning. She sprinkled some water
over her bright pink flower, and climbed into
bed. Doom rubbed her head against Ruby's chin
and then leaped off the bed and into her own.

"Good night, Doom," Ruby said, and within
minutes, she was fast asleep.

Doom did not fare as well. She tossed,
turned, stared at the ceiling, and counted sheep.
She began to think a trip to the kitchen for some
warm milk might be in order, but then suddenly,

something incredible happened. The pink flower on the windowsill . . . began to shake. Then the roots stood up like legs and stepped out of the pot. Next, the plant hopped off the ledge,

onto the floor, and then shuffled out the door. It left a trail of dirt behind. Doom Kitty pretended to be asleep as the flower crept by her, but as soon as the plant left the room, she bolted after it.

Doom followed the plant to the kitchen. From a hiding spot in a dark corner, she watched as the flower used its leaves to open a cupboard. Then it pulled out Ruby's freshly baked loaf of bread and swallowed it in one gulp! Doom rubbed her eyes in disbelief.

Next, the flower found the plate of muffins that Ruby had prepared for breakfast the next day. Sure enough, it ate them all.

When all the food was gone, the flower made a noise that sounded like a burp. It shuffled toward the door, again leaving behind a trail of dirt and leaves. Doom followed it up the stairs, all the way back to Ruby's room. She frantically tried to wake up Ruby by nuzzling her cheek as the flower climbed back up to the windowsill.

"What? What's wrong, Doom?" Ruby asked sleepily. Doom pointed toward the flower, which was now settling back into its pot. Ruby rubbed her eyes and yawned as

Doom frantically pointed toward the window.

Ruby shook her head. "I don't understand, Doom. What is it?" she said sleepily.

Doom opened her mouth wide and waved her arms to the side, like branches of a tree. Then she walked off the bed and shuffled around the floor, pretending to put objects into her mouth. She pointed again to the flower, and then looked up at Ruby.

"We'll have to talk in the morning," Ruby said. "I'm too tired to have a conversation about monkeys right now." Doom leaped back up onto the bed, but Ruby had already fallen back into a deep sleep. Doom sighed, as she had no choice but to try to do the same. She curled up in her bed and tried to rest, but kept one eye on the flower the entire time.

The next morning, Ruby and Doom walked

into the kitchen to find it even more of a mess than the night before. The rest of the gang was already there, looking inside the empty cabinets and drawers, bewildered.

Doom stepped forward and began to act out what the flower had done the previous evening. She opened her mouth wide and pretended to eat everything in sight.

"I think Doom's hungry," said Ruby. "Poor thing. I'll scramble up an egg for you right away."

Doom shook her head, but it was too late. Ruby was already pulling out bowls and skillets, ready to make breakfast not only for her, but for everyone. Doom motioned to Skull Boy instead. She started out in a stationary pose—like the flower in the pot—then slowly stood up and shuffled across the floor to the cupboard where last night's bread and muffins were eaten.

Skull Boy gasped. "Doom isn't saying she's hungry, Ruby." Doom nodded enthusiastically.

"She is confessing to the crime!" he exclaimed. Doom slapped her forehead with her paw.

"Doom, why'd you do it? Did you have an accomplice?" asked Skull Boy.

Doom took a deep breath. She curled up and closed her eyes, to try to show that she had been asleep the previous night. Then she went into the flower routine again.

"Aha! So you were sleepwalking!" Skull Boy said. Doom shook her head, frustrated.

"You were dreaming about sleepwalking?" Iris guessed. Doom shook her head.

"You were awake-walking?" asked Frank. Doom rolled her eyes. She mimed what the flower had done again.

"You were dreaming about awake-walking while monkeys from outer space came down and ate all the food!" Len shouted, sure he had guessed it correctly. Doom let out an exasperated sigh.

Chapter Seven

"Early to bed,
early to rise, makes a kitty
a prime suspect!"

Later that day, Skull Boy resumed his search
for clues. He was not able to figure out what
Doom had been trying to say in the kitchen that
morning, but he was no longer certain that she
was guilty. After all, how could she have eaten
all that food by herself!

So he questioned everyone in the mansion
again. Did anyone besides Scaredy hear strange
noises last night or the night before? Did they
hear voices? Did they see anything unusual
around the mansion? What did they think of
Skull Boy's cool new cape? No one had any

new information, but they all liked the cape very much.

Skull Boy continued to search the house for clues, but all he found was Ruby cleaning up another pile of dirt and leaves in the hallway.

"More dirt?" he asked.

"Yeah, it must have been Iris, tracking dirt in from outside," Ruby said as she swept the large green leaves into a dustpan.

"Couldn't be," said Skull Boy. "Iris has been in the Great Hall all day, practicing her trapeze act."

"Oh, well then, perhaps Frank and Len came in," Ruby guessed.

"Nope," Skull Boy said again. "Frank and Len have been in their garage since breakfast, writing a song for the flower."

"Hmm. Then Misery . . ."

"Making another bowl up in her room."

"Scaredy and Boo Boo?" Ruby wondered.

"Playing hide-and-go-seek in the attic."

"Poe?"

"Still cooped up in his coop. It seems everyone is playing indoors today," Skull Boy said, examining the leaves under his lens.

"Doom has been acting strange lately," Ruby said. "Maybe she brought these leaves in here to tell us something."

"Maybe," Skull Boy agreed. "But what?"

Unable to crack the case by the end of the

day, Skull Boy came up with a plan. He set up an elaborate booby trap in the kitchen. He tied a wire around some pots and pans and then ran the line across the doorway. As soon as the food burglar walked into the room, he or she would trip the wire and cause the pots and pans to come crashing down. Furthermore, Skull Boy rigged the door to lock once the wire was tripped, so the thief would be trapped inside.

Skull Boy didn't even bother to put on his pajamas that night. Instead, he lay awake in bed, waiting for the sound of pots and pans so he could finally nab the culprit.

Doom paced back and forth in front of the windowsill. She was determined to keep an eye on that flower all night long. As the hours passed and the moonlight waned, however, Doom's eyes grew heavy. Still standing guard, she nodded off to sleep.

Sure enough, just as Doom's eyes closed
and her breathing turned into the soft *Zs* of
sleep, the flower stood up. It very quietly, very
carefully, stepped out of its pot and climbed
down from the windowsill. It slipped past Doom
Kitty and Ruby, and headed toward the kitchen.
A few moments later . . .

CRASH BANG CLASH KRUSH BOOM!!!!

Skull Boy's booby trap worked perfectly and
everyone was woken from their slumber. Doom
woke with a jolt, saw the empty flowerpot, and
raced to the kitchen.

"Doom!" shouted Skull Boy as she approached
the kitchen door. "Any remaining doubts I had
about you being the thief are gone."

Just then, Ruby arrived. "Everything okay?"
she asked breathlessly.

"It seems we've caught our thief," said Skull
Boy. "I knew it was Iris all along!"

"What was Iris all along?" Iris called from the top of the stairs. She slid down the banister to meet them. Startled, Skull Boy backtracked and said, "Oh, I meant to say, that is, I knew it was Iris all along who was innocent! But Frank and Len—they're the real culprits. Oh, what a fool I was to believe their story!"

Just then, Frank and Len joined the group. "Hey, everyone," said Frank. "What's all the ruckus?" Ruby, Iris, and Doom looked at Skull Boy and smirked.

"Nothing!" said Skull Boy. "I meant, um, what a fool I was to believe their story about flowers eating ham on rye sandwiches. Preposterous! I knew they weren't the thieves."

Ruby raised an eyebrow at Skull Boy. "Really?" she said. "Then who is?"

"Ah," said Skull Boy, as if certain he had it all figured out now, "you mean, who *are* the thieves? Anyone can see that Scaredy Bat and

Boo Boo have been working together this entire time!"

"Nnnnmph!" came a muffled, high-pitched voice from under the rug. It was Scaredy Bat, hiding. He wiggled out and said, "No, Mr. Detective Skull Boy, sir. It wasn't me. And if you look up, I think you will see that Mr. Boo Boo is quite innocent as well." Skull Boy looked up to see Boo Boo hovering above him.

Poe flew in through the open windows and hovered alongside Boo Boo. Since he was outside the kitchen as well, Poe could not be guilty, either.

"Oh," said Skull Boy, "I apologize. Well, then . . . uh, well, then that leaves only one person who has not shown her face tonight. The criminal must be . . ."

"Misery?" said Misery, shuffling into the room. She stopped and looked at everyone tiredly. "Hi."

"But . . . but . . . if everyone's out here, then who's in there?" Skull Boy asked, looking at the locked kitchen door.

"Time to find out," said Ruby, and she took a large, black iron key out of her pocket and unlocked the door.

Chapter Eight

> "Fish gotta swim,
> birds gotta fly, flowers
> gotta eat pie!"

Ruby opened the door and Skull Boy leaped into the kitchen like a tiger about to pounce on its prey. "Aha! I've caught you! You . . . you . . ." He looked left, right, up, down, and straight ahead, but he didn't see anything out of the ordinary. He especially didn't pay any attention to the flower that sat near the kitchen table.

"Uh, hello?" Skull Boy called.

"Come out, come out, wherever you are!" called Iris.

"Olly olly oxen free!" called Boo Boo.

The others searched the closets and cabinets,

even under the table, but still, it appeared that nobody was there.

Doom rushed over to the flower and pointed frantically. Ruby noticed and said, "Oh, Doom, did you bring our new flower down here for a change of scenery? That was nice."

Doom shook her head. She tried once again to mime the flower's actions, shuffling about the floor with her mouth wide open. But Ruby just thought she was hungry again. "How about I

make us all a midnight snack?" she suggested. "The thief can't have gotten everything."

Sure enough, Ruby found a plate of lemon cookies on one of the shelves, and all the friends took a seat at the table. After taking a cookie, Ruby passed the plate to Iris. Iris took a cookie, then passed the plate to Misery. But when the plate got to Skull Boy, it was empty.

"Hey!" he cried. "Where'd all of Ruby's cookies go?"

Indeed, the once-full plate of lemon cookies was now completely empty! The gang's eyes widened with shock.

Just then, the flower that rested near the table, right between Misery and Skull Boy, burped. Everyone turned to see the flower cover its mouth with one of its leaves, as if to say, "Excuse me." The friends exchanged looks of surprise, and then burst out laughing!

Finally, they had found the guilty party. "But

I don't understand," said Skull Boy. "How can
a flower eat that much? And also, why would
a flower want muffins and buns, anyway? I
thought they absorbed nutrients through the
soil."

Poe walked up to the flower and began to
examine its leaves and petals. "There are always
exceptions, my boy," he said. "Remember the
Venus flytrap?"

Skull Boy nodded.

"Not all plants and flowers are the same," Poe continued. "This particular variety of plant happens to be a *Florus voracious*. They are extremely rare but native to Gloomsville. Their defining characteristics are their large pink petals, and their constant need to eat. They'll eat everything from soup to nuts."

"Cool!" said Len. "So, this flower *would* eat a ham on rye!"

"Are you sure about all this, Poe?" asked Skull Boy.

"Most certainly," asserted Poe. "For the past few days I have been cataloging the flora and fauna of Gloomsville. Fascinating subject, really. *Florus voracious*—a plant that always eats. *Florus vociferous*—a plant that always talks. *Florus vesuvius*—a plant that erupts hot lava once a year. *Florus vagabondus*—a plant that wanders from place to place . . ."

"So this flower isn't really a thief. It's just . . .

hungry?" interrupted Skull Boy.

"That is correct," answered Poe.

"Well, then, I guess 'The Case of the Missing Foodstuffs' is closed," said Skull Boy.

"*Florus voracious,* huh?" considered Ruby. "How about we call her Flora?"

The gang all nodded in agreement.

"Let's let her live in the kitchen, right next to the window. That way, whenever she's hungry she won't have to go far for a snack!"

"Great idea, Ruby!" said Iris.

"Hey—who wants to hear the song we wrote for Flora?" asked Frank.

"I do! I do!" everyone said. They sat at the table and listened while Frank and Len jammed on their electric guitar and sang,

"Hush little flower, don't you cry.
Lenny's gonna feed you a ham on rye!
Hush little flower, don't you fret.
Frank's gonna make you his favorite pet!
Hush little flower, don't you run.
Ruby's gonna bake you a fresh, hot bun!
Hush little flower, we'll be true.
Scaredy Bat's coming to water you!"

As the brothers continued their song, Scaredy Bat and Boo Boo clapped along to the music. Ruby and Iris stood up and started dancing. Skull Boy threw off his cape and leaped up to join the party. Flora bobbed up and down happily, while Poe tapped the tips of his wings on the table to the beat. Even the moon shone more brightly as the music played, and bathed them all in blue light until morning.

Dear Friend,

Were you as surprised as I was that that beautiful little flower turned out to be the midnight snacker? Appearances can be deceiving—that's why you should always take the time to get to know someone, no matter what they look like. After all, you never know when you're going to make a new friend.

Well, that's it for now. But don't worry. My friends and I have many more adventures that we want to share with you.

After all, if you take the road less traveled, you'll find more surprises.

Your friend,

Ruby

Look out for Ruby's next adventure!

Ruby Gloom®
#2 Moon over Gloomsville

There's a lunar eclipse in the skies above Gloomsville, and Ruby and her friends are going camping to watch it. The eclipse causes some very strange things to happen, and soon no one feels quite like themselves anymore! But when Doom Kitty goes missing, will Ruby and the gang be able to overcome the eclipse's effects in time to save her?

Available from Grosset & Dunlap
www.penguin.com/youngreaders